3 Great Offers For Mr Men

1 Token

1 FREE Door Hangers and Posters

In every Mr Men and Little Miss Book like this one [...]
special token. Collect 6 and we will send you either [...]
Men or Little Miss poster and a Mr Men or Little Miss double sided,
full colour, bedroom door hanger. Apply using the coupon overleaf,
enclosing six tokens and a 50p coin for your choice of two items.

[...] towards any
other Egmont World /
World International token
scheme promotions,
in early learning and
story / activity books.

Posters: Tick your preferred choice of either Mr Men ☐ or Little Miss ☐

Door Hangers: Choose from: Mr. Nosey & Mr Muddle ☐, Mr Greedy &
Mr Lazy ☐, Mr Tickle & Mr Grumpy ☐, Mr Slow & Mr Busy ☐, Mr
Messy & Mr Quiet ☐, Mr Perfect & Mr Forgetful ☐, Little Miss Fun &
Little Miss Late ☐, Little Miss Helpful & Little Miss Tidy ☐, Little Miss
Busy & Little Miss Brainy ☐, Little Miss Star & Little Miss Fun ☐.
(Please tick)

2 Mr Men Library Boxes

Keep your growing collection of Mr Men and Little Miss books in
these superb library boxes. With an integral carrying handle and
stay-closed fastener, these full colour, plastic
boxes are fantastic. They are just £5.49 each
including postage. Order overleaf.

3 Join The Club

To join the fantastic Mr Men & Little Miss
Club, check out the page overleaf NOW!

MR MEN and LITTLE MISS™ & © 1998 Mrs. Roger Hargreaves

Join Our Club!

MR. MEN & little miss CLUB

When you become a member of the fantastic Mr Men and Little Miss Club you'll receive a personal letter from Mr Happy and Little Miss Giggles, a club badge with your name, and a superb Welcome Pack (pictured below right).

You'll also get birthday and Christmas cards from the Mr Men and Little Misses, 2 newsletters crammed with special offers, privileges and news, and a copy of the 12 page Mr Men catalogue which includes great party ideas.

If it were on sale in the shops, the Welcome Pack alone might cost around £13. But a year's membership is just £9.99 (plus 73p postage) with a 14 day money-back guarantee if you are not delighted!

HOW TO APPLY To apply for any of these three great offers, ask an adult to complete the coupon below and send it with appropriate payment and tokens (where required) to: Mr Men Offers, PO Box 7, Manchester M19 2HD. Credit card orders for Club membership ONLY by telephone, please call: 01403 242727.

To be completed by an adult

❏ **1.** Please send a poster and door hanger as selected overleaf. I enclose six tokens and a 50p coin for post (coin not required if you are also taking up 2. or 3. below).

❏ **2.** Please send ___ Mr Men Library case(s) and ___ Little Miss Library case(s) at £5.49 each.

❏ **3.** Please enrol the following in the Mr Men & Little Miss Club at £10.72 (inc postage)

Fan's Name:_____Fan's Address:_____

_____Post Code:_____Date of birth:___ /___ /___

Your Name:_____Your Address:_____

_____

Post Code:_____Name of parent or guardian (if not you):_____

Total amount due: £_____ (£5.49 per Library Case, £10.72 per Club membership)

❏ I enclose a cheque or postal order payable to Egmont World Limited.

❏ Please charge my MasterCard / Visa account.

Card number: | | | | | | | | | | | | | | | | |

Expiry Date: _____ /_____   Signature: _____

Data Protection Act: If you do **not** wish to receive other family offers from us or companies we recommend, please tick this box ❏. Offer applies to UK only

little Miss Magic

by Roger Hargreaves

Early one Monday morning in summer, little Miss Magic awoke in the bedroom of Abracadabra Cottage.

Which was where she lived.

She yawned a yawn.

And got out of bed.

She went to the bathroom to clean her teeth.

"Squeeze," she said to the tube of toothpaste.

And, guess what?

The tube of toothpaste jumped up, and squeezed itself on to little Miss Magic's toothbrush.

Honestly!

Little Miss Magic isn't called little Miss Magic for nothing.

When she tells something to do something, it does it!

She went downstairs to the kitchen.

"Boil," she said to the kettle.

And it did!

"Toast," she said to the toaster.

"Spread," she said to a knife.

And the knife jumped up and spread some butter on to the toast.

"Pour," she said to the coffee pot.

And she sat down to breakfast.

Don't you wish you could make things do things like that?

She was enjoying a second cup of coffee when there was a knock at the kitchen door.

"Open," she said to the door.

And, as it did, there stood Mr Happy, looking exactly the opposite.

"You don't look your usual self," remarked little Miss Magic. "What's the matter?"

"Everything," replied Mr Happy.

"Come in and tell me about it," she said.

"Have a cup of coffee."

"Pour," she said to the coffee pot.

"Now," said little Miss Magic. "What is it?"

"It's Mr Tickle," replied Mr Happy. "He's become absolutely impossible!"

"What do you mean?" asked little Miss Magic.

"Well," went on Mr Happy. "He used to go around tickling people every now and then, but now he's going around tickling people all the time!"

He sighed.

Little Miss Magic looked at him.

"It can't be that bad," she said.

"It's worse," said Mr Happy, unhappily.

"Cheer up," she grinned.

"Come on," she said.

And off they set from Abracadabra Cottage.

"After you," said little Miss Magic to Mr Happy.

"Close," she said to the door.

Mr Tickle was in full cry!

What a Monday morning he was having!

He'd tickled Mr Mean until he'd moaned!

And Mr Greedy until he'd groaned!

And little Miss Sunshine until she'd shivered!

And Mr Quiet until he'd quivered!

And little Miss Plump until she'd pleaded!

And little Miss Shy until she'd sobbed!

Not to mention the postman, a policeman, the doctor, three dogs, two cats!

And a worm!

"Aha," cried Mr Tickle as he spied little Miss Magic and Mr Happy.

"Anyone for TICKLES?"

And he rushed up to them, reaching out those extraordinarily long arms of his, with those particularly ticklish fingers on the ends of them.

Little Miss Magic looked at Mr Happy.

"I see what you mean," she said.

And winked.

She pointed at Mr Tickle's extraordinarily long right arm.

"Shrink," she said.

And then she pointed to Mr Tickle's extraordinarily long left arm.

"Shrink," she said again.

And, as you remember, when little Miss Magic tells something to do something, it does it!

Mr Tickle's arms were suddenly not extraordinarily long.

They were extraordinarily ordinary!

"That's not FAIR!" he cried. "You've spoiled my FUN!"

"It might have been fun for you," remarked Mr Happy. "But it wasn't much fun for anybody else."

"Come and see me tomorrow," said little Miss Magic to Mr Tickle.

"There," she said to Mr Happy. "Happy now?"
Mr Happy smiled that famous smile of his.
"I'll say," he said.
"Come on," he added. "I'll buy you lunch."
And off they went to his favourite restaurant.
Smilers!

On Tuesday Mr Tickle went round to Abracadabra Cottage.

He knocked at the front door.

"Open," said a voice inside.

"Oh hello," smiled little Miss Magic as the door opened by itself and she saw who was standing there.

"Come in!"

"I expect you'd like me to make your arms long again?" she said.

"Oh yes please," said Mr Tickle.

"Very well," she said.

Mr Tickle's face lit up.

"On one condition," she added.

His face fell.

"You are only allowed one tickle a day!"

"ONE tickle a DAY?" said Mr Tickle.

"That's not much!"

"Promise," said little Miss Magic.

Mr Tickle sighed.

"Promise," he said.

"Grow," said little Miss Magic.

And both Mr Tickle's arms grew back to their original long length.

"Now don't forget," she reminded him. "One tickle a day!"

"Or else!" she added.

Mr Tickle went out through the door.

"Goodbye," she said to him.

"Shut," she said to the door.

Mr Tickle stood outside little Miss Magic's cottage.

"Ah well," he thought. "One tickle a day is better than no tickles a day!"

It was then that he saw one of the downstairs windows of Abracadabra Cottage was open.

"One tickle a day," he thought.

And a small smile came to his face.

"One tickle a day," he thought.

And, on that Tuesday morning, as one of those extraordinarily long arms reached in through the open window of Abracadabra Cottage, the small smile on the face of Mr Tickle turned into a giant grin.

"One tickle a day," he thought.